WALT DISNEY'S
Lady and the TRAMP

Based on the story
by Ward Greene

Illustrations by
the Walt Disney Studio

A GOLDEN BOOK · NEW YORK
Western Publishing Company, Inc., Racine, Wisconsin 53404

ISBN 0-307-01027-9

LADY was a cocker spaniel who came to live
with two People called Darling and Jim Dear.
She had two neat feeding bowls of her own.
She had a basket with a blanket in it, too.

But she trained her People to feed her from the table—just a bit now and then.

And she trained them to let her sleep at the foot of their beds.

She brought in their morning paper, and most of the mail.

And she ran when Jim Dear whistled, coming home at night.

Lady was sure that she had a very happy home.
And her two next door neighbors, Jock and
Trusty by name, two gentlemanly dogs, agreed
with her.

But there was another dog around the neigh-
borhood, a saucy young fellow called The Tramp.
"I'll wear no man's collar!" was his proud boast.
"That's the way to be happy," said he.

"But where do you sleep?" Lady asked him. "And what do you do for food?"

"Ah, that's easily arranged if you know your way around," said The Tramp with a jaunty air. "And as for you, my proud beauty, you'll find things very different when a baby comes to your house to stay! For there's only so much room for love in People's hearts. And when a baby comes in, out goes the dog!"

His strange words worried Lady. They worried her more when a baby really did come to her house to live. Not that Darling and Jim Dear didn't mean to be kind, but they were very busy now.

And worst of all, Darling's Aunt Sarah came.
"That dog!" she said. "It must stay out in the
yard, and you'll have to have a muzzle for it!"

"Oho!" said The Tramp, when he saw Lady. "So it's happened already, just as I said. Well, I'm sorry to see it, but come along. We'll be rid of that muzzle soon."

"Come along?" cried Lady. "Can't you see I'm tied?"

"I forgot," said The Tramp. "You've a lot to learn." So he showed her how to lunge against the rope until quite soon it broke.

Then away they went, to get the muzzle off.

Lady could not imagine what The Tramp planned, but he led her straight across town, past the guards at the gate of the Zoo.

There they met Beaver.

"Hi there," said The Tramp. "Like to help us out?"

"Sure," said Beaver, "always glad to oblige. Say, Miss, that's a fine muzzle you have there."

"That's just what we want to get rid of," said The Tramp. "You can have it if you get it off."

So Beaver chewed the muzzle off, and when Lady and The Tramp left, after thanking him, he was already trying it on.

"Now where?" said The Tramp. "The world is wide. We'll go anywhere you say."

"Oh, I must go home," said Lady. "I have to watch the house and the baby you know."

"Home!" said The Tramp. "After the muzzle and all? I'll never understand a woman's mind!" But he went along.

Just as they reached Lady's yard they saw a light,
a strange light flickering in the kitchen. It was a
fire, just a little flame, but they knew it should
not be burning there.

"The baby!" cried Lady, and in she raced, with The Tramp right at her heels.

And The Tramp stood guard at the baby's crib,
while Lady woke Jim Dear and Darling.

What a time! When Darling and Jim Dear
woke up, the baby began to cry.

At first Darling and Jim Dear blamed Lady and
The Tramp. But when they saw the fire, all that
was changed.

"Well, thanks, young fellow," said Jim Dear to The Tramp, after he'd put the fire out. "Looks as if you've found yourself a home—and a job. Shall we go down tomorrow for a license and a collar, so everything will be set?"

The Tramp looked out the window where the
wide world waited. Then he looked at Lady at
his side.

"Arf!" he said, which means, "All right." And
he offered Jim a paw to shake.

Now Lady and The Tramp have two families to look after. Darling and Jim Dear and the baby are one.

The other is a family of roly-poly puppies. And The Tramp in his collar is the proudest dog in town.